My Trip to Alpha I

Other Books by Alfred Slote

My Trip to Alpha I

by Alfred Slote

Illustrated by Harold Berson

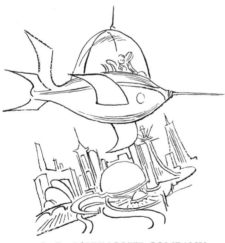

J. B. LIPPINCOTT COMPANY

PHILADELPHIA AND NEW YORK

U.S. Library of Congress Cataloging in Publication Data

Slote, Alfred.
  My trip to Alpha I.

  SUMMARY: VOYA-CODE is the most sophisticated form of interplanetary
travel, but a young boy finds out it is not without dangers.
  [1. Science fiction] I. Berson, Harold. II. Title.
PZ7.S635My   [Fic]   78-6463
ISBN-0-397-31810-3

TO HETSY

1

I NEEDED A TRIP to Alpha I like a hole in the head. But my father said someone had to go there and help Aunt Katherine DeVanter pack and get ready to move back to Earth, and she had specifically asked for me.

"That's terrible," I said. "It'll take me months to get there and back. Basketball season starts soon. My team needs me."

I was captain of the sixth-grade basketball team, but that wasn't important to my father.

He said, "You'll only be gone a week or ten days at the most. Your Aunt Katherine DeVanter is a very wealthy lady, and she has sent us money for you to go by VOYA-CODE."

I stared at him. "Are you serious?"

"Yes, indeed. You'll be the first member of our family who has ever traveled by VOYA-CODE. Are you interested now?"

I guess I was. We'd all taken rocket trips to the Moon and to different planets, and Dad had taken the Superrockets to Alpha Galaxy and Kappa Galaxy on business trips that took months. But just a couple of years ago the scientists had come up with a new way of traveling—VOYA-CODE.

I thought it was kind of a scary idea, but everyone who'd made one of the trips swore by them. A kid in our school who had gone to Jupiter by VOYA-CODE told us it was easier than walking down the stairs. "All you do is get wired up to the Coding Computer. Then someone gives you a shot that puts you to sleep. When you wake up, you're there. It's the only way to travel," this kid said.

I understood how it worked because when VOYA-CODE started, our teacher told us it was really just like a lot of other things in our lives only more so, because now it was being applied to people. The idea began long ago in the twentieth century, when engineers made computer programs of everything: cars, wheels, chairs, tables—and then animals, and finally people.

There was a lot of trouble when they started making computer programs of people. People said you couldn't do that, that a man or a woman was more than a bunch of numbers and equations. But pretty soon the engineers were making computer programs of people that told you what they looked like and how they acted—and even how they felt about things!

The next step was logical enough. Engineers, working from the equations, constructed dummies that looked exactly like the people. When you put computer cards with the right data into the dummies, they became the people!

There were all kinds of riots on Earth and on Mars and Uranus, because people said you wouldn't know whether you were really you, or a dummy programmed to be you. Everything could get mixed up. It was inhuman, they said.

Maybe it was, but it sure had good things going for it. You could send the data by neutro waves to every part of the universe. And then, instead of you taking a long trip by rocket or Superrocket yourself, you could travel by VOYA-CODE. Your computer program would be fed into a dummy that looked just like you and had been made on the planet you were going to. The instant that hap-

pened, the dummy would come alive. The dummy would be you! Meanwhile, back home, your original body would be kept in Sleep-Storage until you were ready to return. Then your dummy would be deprogrammed, all the data would be let out of it, and you'd wake up back home.

The only thing wrong with traveling by VOYA-CODE was that you couldn't move your real self permanently that way, or carry things with you. And so to move back to Earth, Aunt Katherine would have to travel with her

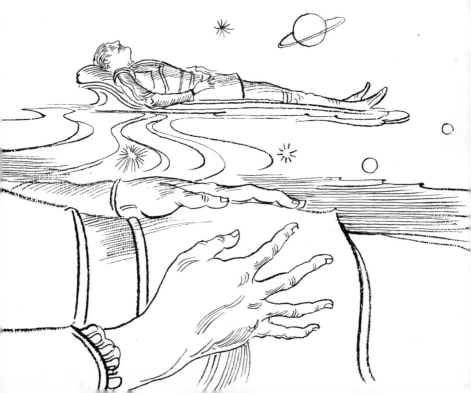

clothes and furniture on the Superrocket. She would get here weeks after I got back.

I would be going six million light years from Earth to Alpha just to help someone pack! But Dad pointed out that that was what Aunt Katherine had requested. And she had specifically asked for *me* to come—not Dad, not Mom, not my sister Jan, who's two years older than me.

It seemed a strange reason to take such a long trip. I didn't like it. But like it or not, I was going.

2

THE WHOLE FAMILY—Mom, Dad, and Jan—
came down to the VOYA-CODE terminal to see
me off. There were lots of people leaving for
different parts of the universe, and it was the
darndest terminal building I'd ever seen. No
loading docks, no ramps, no great Superrockets with their huge power units purring,
waiting to take off. Nothing like that at all.

Just a lot of little rooms. Like a hospital.

"Jack Stevenson to Alpha Galaxy, Alpha I,
Nottingham City," Dad said into the Reception-Microphone.

We heard the tumblers click as the computer cards located my file. And then the

computer voice said: "Terminal Room 8A."

We found Terminal Room 8A just down the hall. It was like no terminal room you ever saw. It was more like a doctor's waiting room. There were chairs and pictures on the walls and people sitting around reading magazines or watching programs on the Vue-Screen.

"This is definitely weird," Jan said.

"I wonder what they're waiting for," I said.

"I'm waiting for my VOYA-CODE to Uranus," a lady said.

"I'm waiting to go to Pluto," a man said.

Everyone was going somewhere, but it still reminded me more of a doctor's office than an interplanetary travel terminal.

One by one the patients—I mean the travelers—were called out by a woman in a white coat. More people came in. Finally the woman called my name.

"This way, please," she said.

"Can we come with him?" my mother asked.

"You can stay with the Traveler till departure time," the woman said. "Then you must leave."

"It's not weird, it's kooky," Jan said.

We followed the woman down a corridor past a lot of little rooms. You couldn't see into the rooms. Finally she led me into a room that said ALPHA I on the door.

It was a little rectangular green room. In the middle was a table with a pillow on it. Above the table was a big light. It was just like the operating room of a hospital. On the walls were pictures of Alpha I. The nurse—I mean the Travel Attendant—escorted me around the room, having me look at the pictures.

"In case you've never been to Alpha before. Of course, you'll wake up in a room exactly like this, and I expect your friends and relatives will be waiting for you." Then I lay down and she hooked me up to the Coding Computer.

My mother looked worried. "How long will it take him to get there?" she asked the Attendant.

"He'll be in Alpha before you're out of the terminal here," the lady said. "Now just lie down, Jack."

"Say hello to Aunt Katherine, Jack," Dad said.

"Have a safe trip," Mom said.

"Can we see him after he goes?" Jan asked.

"Of course not," the Attendant said. "Your brother won't be here, you know."

"Well," Jan said, "his body will."

"Yes, but it will be deprogrammed in Sleep-Storage until he's ready to come back. There's really nothing to worry about. We send out hundreds of travelers every day. You'd better say good-bye now."

"Good-bye, Mom. Good-bye, Dad. Good-bye, Jan."

"Good-bye, Jack," Dad said.

"Good-bye, Jack," Mom said.

"So long, Jack," Jan said.

Then they were gone. I felt a slight sting on my right forearm. And the next thing I knew I was out.

Asleep. A very pleasant sleep. I didn't

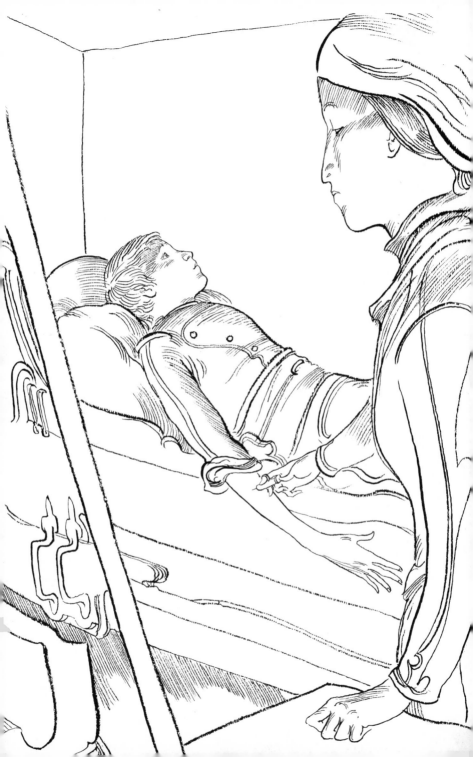

dream about trips or galaxies or anything fancy. I dreamt about my basketball team. I was dribbling down the court and everyone was shouting, "Go, Jack. Go, Jack. Go!"

I went floating through the air like a bird, high above the crowd, high above the backboard, higher and higher and higher, and people were yelling, "Jack, come on back. Jack!"

3

"HELLO, JACK," Aunt Katherine DeVanter said. "Welcome to Alpha I."

I opened my eyes and there she was: tall, red-headed, with sharp eyes that looked right into your heart.

"Hello, Aunt Katherine," I replied. "How are you?"

"Listen to him," she said. "The child travels over six million light years to visit me and he asks me how *I* am. I am fine, thank you. The question is: How are you? What did your trip feel like?"

I laughed. "Like taking a nap."

"Wonderful! That means he's ready to leave for my ranch right away."

Aunt Katherine was talking to a woman in white—the twin of the woman in white back at the VOYA-CODE terminal on Earth, the Travel Attendant. In fact, I thought, looking about, everything was exactly as it had been on Earth. The same green room, the table . . . the only difference was a sign that said:

WELCOME TO ALPHA I
A GOOD PLACE TO VISIT

The Alpha Travel Attendant said, "We do like our voyagers to wait just a few minutes, Mrs. DeVanter, while we confirm that their parts are all in working order."

"What parts?" I asked. I felt like me. My skin felt like flesh. I knew I was inside a dummy, but in my head it felt like me.

"Your heart, your computer program, your—"

"Well, all right," Aunt Katherine interrupted impatiently, "but hurry along—we must be off. I'm a busy woman with a lot to do. Get your nonsense over with, young lady."

That was Aunt Katherine DeVanter for you. She thought she could order everyone around. I guess when you're old and rich you think you can do anything.

"This will just take a few seconds, Mrs. DeVanter," the Travel Attendant said. She then hooked me up to a bunch of machines, and on a Vue-Screen I saw all kinds of waves and dots.

"Heartbeat normal," the Travel Attendant said, and made a note on a paper.

"Brain scan perfect," she said, and made another note.

"Blood pressure off one thousandth. Nothing to worry about. All in all, a beautiful reading."

"Do I have real blood inside me?" I asked the Travel Attendant.

"Of course you have real blood," Aunt Katherine said. "You're in a perfect dummy, Jack. I paid a fortune for it. There's no way anyone could tell which you is the *real* you."

"I'm afraid there is one way," the Travel

Attendant said. She took my hand and put it on the small of my back. I felt a little ridge of skin, like a scar, about five inches long.

"What's that?" I asked.

"That's your CES—your Computer Entry Scar. That's where your computer program was inserted, Jack, and *that* is the only difference between you here on Alpha and your body back on Earth."

"Enough of that," Aunt Katherine said quickly. "I like him the way he is. And now we must be leaving."

"You can sit up now, Jack," the Travel Attendant said. "How do you feel?"

"Fine."

"You're ready to leave the terminal. We thank you for taking VOYA-CODE to Alpha."

I stood up and started to go over to give Aunt Katherine a hug and a kiss. After all, I'd come a very long way to see her. And in our family we do a lot of hugging and kissing. Aunt Katherine on her visits to Earth always used to hug us a lot, saying we were

23

her only living relatives "anywhere in the universe."

So I went over to hug her.

To my surprise, she backed away from me.

"We really must get going, dear," she said. "We have lots to do before you go back to Earth."

And without another word, without even shaking my hand, Aunt Katherine DeVanter bustled out the door. It was odd. What was the big hurry?

As I went out behind her, I heard the Travel Attendant say into a microphone:

"This is VOYA-CODE, Alpha I, Nottingham City. Jack Stevenson has arrived safely from Earth. All working parts in order."

I hurried to catch up with Aunt Katherine.

4

MOMENTS LATER we were winging our way in the sunlight over Nottingham City. There were hundreds of solar craft in the air, and Aunt Katherine kept up a running commentary on the driving habits of others.

"Look at that idiot! Who ever gave him a license to fly? Get out of the way."

I certainly didn't remember Aunt Katherine being so jumpy on Earth. When she visited us she seemed very relaxed; she always had time for stories about when she and Uncle Rudolph were pioneers on Alpha I and how hard things were. My picture of Alpha I was a land of uranium mines run by strong-minded women like Aunt Katherine and quiet, brave men like Uncle Rudolph.

Now I had the opportunity to look around Alpha for myself. The city below us was a city of golden towers and ramps. Real gold. Nottingham was one of the wealthiest cities in the universe; Alpha I with all its mines was one of the wealthiest planets.

We flew over a river that circled the city and then we were over forests and streams and huge farming bubbles in which the temperature was kept exactly right for the crops. Robot farmers were working in the fields.

It looked grand to me, but Aunt Katherine started complaining about how the planet was going to pot. How no one worked hard anymore. Robots had been perfected to such a degree that now *they* wanted pleasures too. Although, she added, her Arbos didn't spoil the mining robots of DeVanter Mining Enterprises, Ltd.

I was curious about what Arbos were. I was sure I would soon find out.

After a while the plastic-covered farms dis-

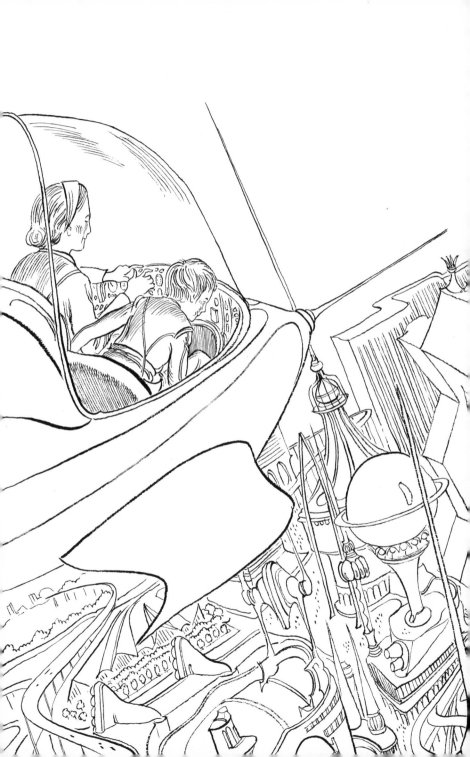

appeared and the land got hilly, and we were over mining country. Huge uranium and titanium mines—and they, like the farms, were encased in plastic domes. The domes controlled the air that was fed down to the robot miners. These were accident-free mines, Aunt Katherine said proudly, and they were very, very profitable.

"Did you know it would be safe to live here when you and Uncle Rudolph first came?" I asked her.

Aunt Katherine, who usually liked to talk about the old days on Alpha, looked at me blankly. "Why . . . I don't remember."

She'd remembered when she'd visited us on Earth. I'd practically become the Alpha expert of my school because of all the stories Aunt Katherine had told us.

I knew that centuries and centuries ago mining operations had been removed from our worn-out old Earth and relocated on different planets in the universe. Alpha I had been one of those planets, and it was only in the last thirty or so years that people with no connection with the mines had come here to settle.

In that time, Aunt Katherine and her late husband, Mr. Rudolph DeVanter, had become two of the wealthiest inhabitants of Alpha. Aunt Katherine used to say that Uncle Rudolph "had a nose for finding new mines and an even better nose for getting people to help run them."

The solar craft she was steering dipped down and we flew over a huge sign carved on a rock surface that said:

DEVANTER MINING ENTERPRISES, LTD.

"That's us, isn't it?" I asked.

"That's *me*," Aunt Katherine corrected.

I had to laugh—she was certainly blunt. She laughed too. "You must forgive an old woman, Jack. I haven't been sleeping too well lately."

For someone who hadn't been sleeping well, she certainly flew a fast and steady course. I wished she'd slow down. I was fascinated by what lay below.

Below us and ahead of us, as far as the eye could see, the plastic mining domes filled the horizon. Pollution-free mining.

"Do you really own all these mines, Aunt Katherine?"

"All these and more, my boy. Many more."

Her eyes gleamed. Well, I guess you don't get as rich as she was by not being a little bit greedy. But if she was so greedy, why was she selling everything and moving back to Earth?

A landing signal sounded on our instrument panel. Below us I saw her ranch. Her house was a long, low, white building with solar heat receivers on the roofs. There were trees all around it and, in the center of the grounds, a big swimming pool. Dad had told us that Aunt Katherine loved to swim.

Not far from the pool was a circular landing pad with a ramp for engaging and securing solar craft. I could see two people down there; they were looking up at us.

"And there are my loyal Arbos," Aunt Katherine said.

"What are Arbos?" I asked this time.

She laughed. "The Arbos are very dear people who comforted me after my darling Rudolph died. They're Alpha natives who have worked for us for years. I don't know what I would have done without them."

"What do you do *with* them, Aunt Katherine?"

"Don't be fresh, young man. Frank Arbo manages my mines for me, and Ruth Arbo manages the house. They are a perfect couple, and all these years I have paid them next to nothing. But I am going to make up for that—I intend to leave all the DeVanter mines to them."

"Oh?"

"That's correct. I have quite enough money to live happily on Earth, and Frank and Ruth deserve my mines."

I got a closer look at Frank and Ruth Arbo as our aircraft dipped toward the landing pad. They stood there, holding hands, smiling up at us. As though they were waiting for money to fall from heaven into their laps.

Which, I guess, it was doing.

"In fact," Aunt Katherine added as the landing legs came out, "one of the first things you can do for me, my dear Jack, is to witness the transfer of my mines to Frank and Ruth."

"Me?"

"Yes, my dear, you."

We landed. She turned off the power and pushed the button marked RAMP. The signal-guided ramp moved toward us.

"According to the laws of Alpha, all sales and transfers of property must be witnessed by a member of the family. You will be representing the family."

The thing was, I was the youngest in the family. It seemed strange. No one back home had mentioned anything about my witnessing a legal document. They must not have known.

I didn't have time to think any more about it. The ramp had hooked onto our craft and the door had swung open and there in the

doorway, beaming at us, were two of the
strangest people I'd ever had the bad luck to
meet.

5

FRANK AND RUTH ARBO looked at me with fixed smiles on their lips. But there was nothing friendly about the careful way they examined me. I felt like a fish they had just caught.

Aunt Katherine seemed to like them. "Jack," she said, "I want you to meet the two most wonderful people in the world—Frank and Ruth Arbo."

"Oh, Master Jack, your aunt is too kind," Frank Arbo said, beaming.

"Mrs. DeVanter has been so good to us," said Ruth Arbo, and she was beaming too.

They were like a pair of robots, the way

they spoke, each echoing the other. As if they had rehearsed every line.

"And we are so glad to meet you, Master Jack," Frank said. "Your aunt has told us so much about you."

"And all very good, Master Jack," added Ruth.

"We're so glad you've come here to help Mrs. DeVanter get ready to move to Earth," Frank said.

"How kind of you to come all this way to help her."

"Perhaps you're tired and would like to lie down."

"Or have something to eat. I could fix you your favorite food, Master Jack."

"Or drink."

"Perhaps you'd like a swim in the pool."

"Your wish is our command," concluded Frank Arbo.

My wish was for both of them to go jump in an Alpha lake. But I didn't say it. Dad always says I pop off too fast. He says he'll know I'm growing up when I don't always say right away what I'm thinking.

I started growing up that very moment on Alpha I.

"What did I tell you, Jack?" Aunt Katherine said, and *she* beamed at me. "Aren't they simply wonderful?"

I decided to smile too. Immediately they began bustling about, showing me the ranch house, the room I'd sleep in, my Vue-Screen that could take in programs from neighboring planets. They showed me where my bathroom was and how I could call any robot servant I wanted on the service console.

They were all over me. I had the feeling I was being watched rather than welcomed.

The tour of the house became especially interesting when we got to the Control Center situated right in the middle of the house. From it, all of the DeVanter Mining Enterprises were run.

It was a circular room with lots of Vue-Screens, computers, data-card machines, and about a thousand control switches. Frank Arbo explained how he controlled every operation for every mine that Aunt Katherine owned.

"Altogether we can activate over twenty-five thousand robot miners from this room. We own more than one thousand uranium and titanium mines on Alpha."

I wondered about that "we" and remembered how Aunt Katherine had corrected me when I'd said those mines all belonged to "us," but she didn't correct Frank Arbo.

After the tour we had supper. It was served by robot servants who were supervised by Ruth Arbo.

"I hope you like vegetables, Master Jack," Ruth Arbo said.

Ugh, I thought. But the vegetables that were served were like none I'd ever seen on Earth. One looked like a carrot crossed with a tomato and you ate it like corn on the cob, holding each end of the carrot. It tasted great.

Ruth Arbo explained that the vegetables

were raised on and flown in from their experimental satellite farm in space.

Frank Arbo asked me what I thought of Alpha I.

"It's very nice," I said honestly. "I didn't think it was going to be so pretty, or that the food would taste so good."

The truth was that, in spite of Aunt Katherine's tales and the travel-poster pictures, I had expected Alpha I to be full of smoke and industry.

Frank Arbo's eyes gleamed.

"Ah, but it is we who have made it pretty, Master Jack. You people on Earth assigned Alpha I to be a work planet for you, to feed you minerals and energy. It was we who slaved in the depths of our land and out of ugliness created beauty. It is *we,* not you Earthlings, who made Alpha such a rich and beautiful place to live. It is *we*—"

"Frank," Ruth Arbo said warningly, "Master Jack doesn't want to hear the history of our planet, do you, Master Jack?"

40

"Sure I do. History is almost my favorite subject in school."

Frank Arbo laughed. He was calm again. "No, Master Jack, Ruth is right. History is for old people. To youth belongs the future, is that not right, Mrs. DeVanter?"

"Not quite right, Frank," Aunt Katherine said in a quiet, precise voice. "The future also belongs to you. I have taken the liberty, dear Frank, of telling Jack about my intention of turning the DeVanter Mining Enterprises over to you and Ruth. And Jack was delighted, weren't you, dear?"

I didn't remember being delighted, but I nodded. I didn't know what else to do.

Frank and Ruth Arbo looked pleased.

"You're more than kind, Mrs. DeVanter."

"And always so generous to us," Ruth added.

"And, my darling Arbos, Jack is willing to be the family witness as required by Alpha law."

"Oh, Master Jack is more than kind himself," said Frank.

"And so generous for one so young," said Ruth.

They were laying it on a little thick, I thought.

"You know, I never believe in putting things off," Aunt Katherine said. "Frank, will you get those legal papers for me right now?"

"Of course, Mrs. DeVanter," Frank Arbo said obediently.

In just a few seconds he was back with a stack of papers.

"Now, Jack, if you'll sign your name here . . . and put your address there."

I didn't seem to have much choice, so I signed.

Jack Stevenson
_____
FAMILY WITNESS

1212 Metro A-1
_____
ADDRESS

New Jersey
_____

Earth
_____

Then Aunt Katherine signed the papers.

And finally the Arbos, looking very solemn, also signed.

"There," said Aunt Katherine, "it's done." She suddenly looked tired.

"And now," she said, "if you'll excuse me. I am exhausted. I think I'll be going to bed."

"I'm sure Master Jack is tired too," Ruth Arbo said. "After such a long trip."

I wasn't tired. Traveling by VOYA-CODE wasn't tiring. But I didn't see much point in staying up with those two birds.

So I went to bed too.

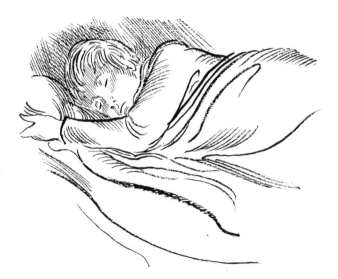

6

THAT NIGHT, my first night in Alpha Galaxy, I had a wild dream. I dreamt that I was flying alone in space, somewhere between the VOYA-CODE terminal on Earth and the VOYA-CODE terminal on Alpha I. I was looking for my body. Spaceships passed by and people stared out through lighted windows. They were staring right through me. I had to go on looking for my body.

Then, all of a sudden, I was on a table and a Travel Attendant in a white uniform was saying to me, "This will hurt for just a second, Jack. Then you'll be yourself again. There. Now take a look."

45

She was holding a mirror out for me to look into.

I looked into the mirror. Staring back at me was the face of Frank Arbo, with its beady eyes and unreal smile.

It was enough to wake anyone up. When I awoke, I realized I had been sleeping on my stomach. Dad says you never dream if you sleep on your stomach. That may be true on Earth, but here on Alpha, anything seemed possible.

Just to make sure, though, that I *was* on Alpha, I reached my hand around to my back and touched it. It was still there—the thin ridge of skin, the scar where they had inserted the computer program. I *was* on Alpha I; I *was* in a dummy programmed to be me. I was supposed to help Aunt Katherine pack her things for her return to Earth. But she was behaving strangely. She acted as if the most important reason for my visit was to help her give away all her mines to those Arbos.

The moment I thought of the Arbos I knew I'd made a mistake, because I couldn't get

SUNMAN ELEM. SCHOOL
SUNMAN, INDIANA 47041

back to sleep. I didn't want to dream I'd turned into Frank Arbo again, so I lay there with my eyes open and listened to the sounds of Aunt Katherine's house.

Back home, our floors creak, our doors creak, and you can always hear the steady whirr of the nuclear power pack in our basement.

But here it was silent except for funny clicking noises. Were they part of an Alpha power system? They seemed to be coming from the middle of the house.

I got out of bed and opened my door a crack. The clicking noises were coming from Aunt Katherine's Control Center—or, I guess I should say, the Arbos' Control Center.

I tiptoed down the hall. A blue light glowed in the Control Center. I heard two people talking in low voices: Frank and Ruth Arbo. Could they be running the DeVanter mines all night long too?

Frank was saying, "We must keep programming it. We must stay ahead."

And Ruth Arbo said, "I'm worried. I don't think we have enough input data."

"It's not a question of input data," he replied. "It's a question of counter-programming."

"We don't know enough," she said.

"We must keep at it anyway," he said.

He must have pushed a bunch of buttons then, because there were a lot more clicks, and I could see red and green lights switching on and off and then computer cards falling into different slots.

Alpha was full of mysteries. I started to go back to my room. I must have made a noise, because Ruth Arbo said:

"Did you hear something, Frank?"

"Nothing but these computers."

I froze. Why, I didn't know. The Arbos were only doing their job—running the mines. What difference did it make if I caught them at it in the middle of the night? Aunt Katherine would only say they were being extra loyal, working overtime. But just the same, something inside me told me it would not be good if they found I had been listening.

"It must be my imagination," Ruth Arbo said at last. "You know, Frank, I'll be glad when this is all over."

"It is *almost* over," Frank said. "We're past the worst of it."

The worst of what? I wondered. But I didn't

hang around to think about it. I tiptoed back to bed.

"Wake up, you sleepy Earthling," Aunt Katherine said as she pulled up the shades and the sun flooded my room. It was going to be a hot day on Alpha I.

"Good morning, Aunt Katherine."

"Good afternoon, you mean. It's practically noon. Your trip to Alpha I took more out of you than you thought. Well, what's my nephew's pleasure today? What would he like to do?"

"He'd like to help you get ready for your trip to Earth, Aunt Katherine."

"Nonsense. It's much too hot to pack. You have some lunch and take a swim in the pool."

"Will you come swimming too?"

She looked as though I'd suggested the worst thing in the world. "I certainly won't. I dislike swimming."

"Huh?" I was flabbergasted. Dad had said she loved to swim. And why else would she have had a pool built?

"Besides, I have lots of things to do."

Looking annoyed, she left the room. I wished my sister Jan were here so we could talk this over. It was weird. I mean, I hadn't made this trip to take a dip in a pool. I'd come to help Aunt Katherine get ready to return to Earth. But she didn't act like someone who wanted to leave.

I dressed and went to lunch. Robot servants served me, cleaned up; robot servants were outside gardening. The Arbos were not around. Well, they had to sleep sometime.

I didn't know what to do, so I ended up doing what Aunt Katherine had suggested—I went swimming. There was even a swimsuit hanging in my room. Aunt Katherine had thought of everything—except why she'd brought me here.

I wondered if the water would get into my Computer Entry Scar, but it didn't; the scar was absolutely waterproof. Every once in a while I'd reach around and touch it, feeling the thin ridge of skin, reminding myself that this was no dream—that I really was going swimming on Alpha.

At about three in the afternoon Aunt Katherine came out of the house, looking tired.

"Come on, Aunt Katherine. The water's fine. Let's go swimming," I called out to her.

She went right back inside the house.

The Arbos weren't at supper with us that night. They were busy in the Control Center with their computers. Aunt Katherine sat across the table from me, and, again, I thought she looked tired.

"Are you OK, Aunt Katherine?" I asked.

"Of course I am," she said.

"You don't look well."

"I *am* well."

"Sorry. Do you know when you'll be leaving for Earth?"

It was a very simple and logical question. But you'd have thought I'd asked her to name the day of her death.

"Leaving for Earth?" she repeated.

"Yes, leaving for Earth. That's why I came here, isn't it? To help you get ready to leave? Dad said that's why you sent for me. Aren't you going to move back to Earth?"

She hesitated and then said, "Jack, I have decided to postpone my move for a while."

"Why?"

More hesitation. Then: "I am not ready to go yet."

"Gee, Aunt Katherine. I think you're ready. You're more than ready. What's keeping you here? You've turned all your mines over to the Arbos. Why stay now?"

"I am not ready to go yet," she repeated.
"Why not?"

"I am not ready to go yet," she said for the third time.

"Aunt Katherine, look at me. What's the matter?"

She looked like she was ready to collapse.

"Aunt Katherine, I *know* something's wrong. If Dad were here, he'd know what to do. I'm pretty young, but I can help. What's the matter? What's going on in this place? It doesn't feel right to me. Those Arbos, I don't think they're such nice people. Is that what's bothering you?"

Panic fluttered in her eyes. Her hands moved jerkily, as though they were being pulled by strings.

"Aunt Katherine," I said, and I got up and ran around the table and put my arms around her and finally gave her the hug I should have given her at the VOYA-CODE terminal.

"I can help you, Aunt Katherine. I can—"

I froze. With my arms around her, my right hand was touching the small of her back

56

and I felt something that was both strange
and familiar.

A small ridge of skin, about five inches
long.

I jumped back.

"You're not Aunt Katherine," I said.

She burst into tears.

7

MY FIRST IMPULSE was to hug her again to make her stop crying. But what good would that do? She wasn't Aunt Katherine. I mean, she was less herself than I was myself.

My second impulse was to make her tell me where her real body was. But would she know?

My third impulse was to find someone else to talk to and tell him what I'd discovered. But the only other people around were the Arbos. And suppose the Arbos already knew?

I shuddered. I was alone in a strange galaxy with strange people. I had to be cool and careful.

So I sat there at the table and tried to sort it out. The ridge of skin—the Computer Entry Scar—that was why she hadn't let me hug her at the VOYA-CODE terminal on my arrival. It was probably also why she wouldn't put on a swimsuit and go swimming.

All right, she was in a dummy, the way I was. But she wasn't functioning well. Someone had botched her programming. Someone was probably programming her illegally. She shouldn't even exist here on her home planet as a dummy. The dummies were supposed to be on the planets you were visiting.

That was as far as I got when Aunt Katherine stopped crying and said quietly, "I'm so sorry."

"It's not your fault," I said. "Anyway, everything's going to be all right."

"I don't think so," she said. "I'm very afraid."

"Aunt Katherine, do you know where the real you is?"

She shook her head.

"Can you remember anything at all?"

She thought for a moment. "I can remember . . . I was somewhere else once. Someplace very different."

"Where was it?"

"I don't know. It's been blocked out. But then I was taken from that place and brought here. Oh, I'm so confused and so tired. Every night they put a new program in me. New data. I'm tired and I'm nervous. And now I'm running down."

"Who's *they,* Aunt Katherine? Who is doing this to you?"

She hesitated. She was afraid to say.

"Is it the Arbos?" I asked.

She nodded. "They've programmed me to love them, and to give them all my mines, but the data doesn't work all the time, and I get so jumpy and exhausted."

So that, I thought, was what Frank and Ruth Arbo were up to at night in the Control Center. They weren't looking after the De-Vanter Mining Enterprises, which they had just stolen. They were frantically trying to

keep Aunt Katherine's dummy programmed. And they were doing a very bad job of it.

Only the VOYA-CODE people could program correctly. Why, only the VOYA-CODE people could have made such a *real* dummy in the first place!

I thought about that for a moment. If the VOYA-CODE people had made Aunt Katherine's dummy, it meant that Aunt Katherine had been planning a VOYA-CODE trip, probably to visit us on Earth. And of course her dummy had been constructed on Earth, where it had been waiting for its computer program to be forwarded from Alpha.

The Arbos must have taken a rocket ship to Earth, kidnapped Aunt Katherine's dummy from a VOYA-CODE factory or from storage, and brought the dummy back to Alpha for their own purposes.

And that meant—I could feel excitement rising inside me—that meant that my *real* Aunt Katherine had to be still here on Alpha I, in Nottingham City, in the VOYA-CODE terminal, in Alpha/Earth Sleep-Storage!

I sat there and let the bits and pieces of my discovery settle into place. Everything fitted together.

After they got her dummy to Alpha, and with her real self out of the way in Sleep-Storage, the Arbos began to change the original VOYA-CODE programming. They used Aunt Katherine's own computers, and they reprogrammed her to give them the whole of DeVanter Mining Enterprises, Ltd. Then they sent for me as the family witness. Me, because I was the youngest in the family, the least familiar with Aunt Katherine, and probably the easiest one to fool.

What a clever and evil couple they were.

All right, so far so good. But now that you know, Jack Stevenson—what do you do?

What I had to do was find Aunt Katherine's body and inform the VOYA-CODE people about what had happened.

How do you do that?

I didn't know. It's a lot easier to figure out things than to do something about them.

"Jack," Aunt Katherine said, "I'm getting

so tired again. I can barely keep my eyes open."

She was running out of data.

"Go to bed, Aunt Katherine. I'll see you in the morning."

I didn't stay up much longer either. I didn't want to run into either of the Arbos just yet. They might be able to tell I knew something I shouldn't know. The best thing for me to do was to go to bed and figure out a plan.

Which is what I did. I turned off the lights and lay down and stared at the ceiling. From the Control Center I heard the frantic clicking of computers.

They thought they were almost out of it. They just had to keep programming her until I left for Earth. Then they could have the dummy take to a sickbed while Aunt Katherine's real body stayed in VOYA-CODE storage forever.

It was clear that I had to get to VOYA-CODE storage as soon as possible. And I'd have to take the dummy Aunt Katherine with me.

Before I went to sleep I thought of a fool-proof way to get us both there.

8

IN THE MORNING Aunt Katherine was not up for breakfast, but the ever-smiling Arbos were.

"And how are you today, Master Jack?" Frank Arbo asked me, beaming.

"Fine, thank you."

"Would Master Jack like some more orange juice?" Ruth Arbo asked.

"No, thank you. Isn't Aunt Katherine going to eat with us?"

"Ahem," said Frank. "I'm afraid your aunt isn't feeling too well today. And we think it's best for her to stay in bed today." He cleared his throat again. "By the way, Master Jack, did she mention to you that she won't be going to Earth for a while?"

"Yes, she did," I said, and pretended I didn't care what Aunt Katherine did or did not do. "And I've really got to get back home. I can't wait around till she's made up her mind to go. I'm captain of my basketball team and we have to practice. Is it OK with you if I go back today?"

Was it ever OK with them! They were delighted with my impatience to get back home—but they pretended it made them sad.

"Oh, we will be sorry to see you leave, Master Jack," Ruth Arbo said.

I bet you will be, I thought. I said, "Could Aunt Katherine take me to the VOYA-CODE terminal today?"

They glanced at 'each other. They must have planned to make Aunt Katherine stay in her sickbed until they had got rid of me.

"I'm not sure your aunt is well enough for a trip to the terminal," Frank said.

"Oh, then I'd better not leave till she gets

better. I couldn't leave knowing she was so sick. My father would never forgive me."

More quick looks were exchanged between them.

"Well," Frank Arbo said, "perhaps she might be feeling better by this afternoon."

"Boy, I hope so. I sure want to go home."

"I'll make your reservation," Ruth Arbo said with a smile. "I'm sure Mrs. DeVanter will be able to see you off."

So, after breakfast, Ruth Arbo made the reservation for my trip back to Earth, and shortly before noon Aunt Katherine emerged from her bedroom. Her eyes were bright. They must have zapped her with instant data. Well, I hoped it would last till we found her real body.

"How do you feel, Aunt Katherine?"

"Much better, thank you, Jack," she said carefully. "Thanks to dear Frank and Ruth. They do take such good care of me."

"Ah, you are much too kind to us, Mrs. DeVanter," Frank Arbo said.

Here we go again, I thought.

I interrupted, "Do you know that I'm going back to Earth today, Aunt Katherine?"

"Yes, Jack. Frank and Ruth have told me. I want you to tell your father how grateful I am that he let you come to Alpha. And please tell him that I hope to be visiting Earth in the near future."

A pretty, well-programmed speech. It came from the bottom of her hastily prepared computer cards.

"I'll tell him, Aunt Katherine. Are you ready to take me to the terminal?"

"Yes."

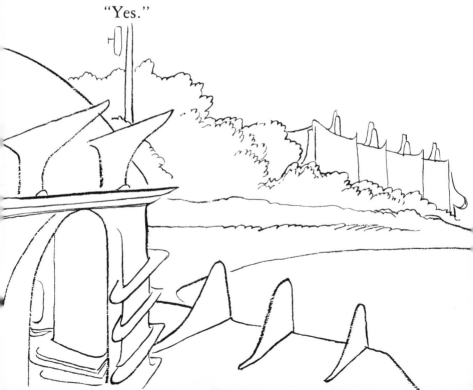

"Then I'll say good-bye to Frank and Ruth."

"Not yet," Frank said with a smile. "Ruth and I are coming with you."

"Oh?"

"Of course, Master Jack," Ruth Arbo chimed in. "We wouldn't dream of not seeing you off."

"But," I said desperately, "you really don't have to."

"But we do," Frank Arbo said, and he went to start the solar craft.

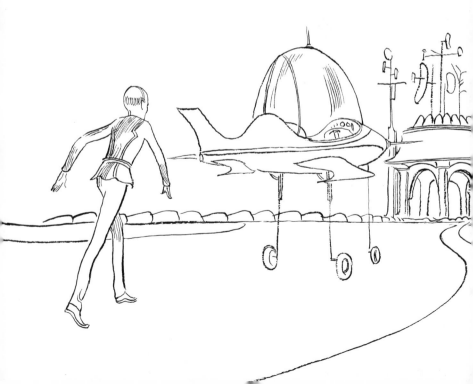

9

THE TRIP TO THE VOYA-CODE terminal in Nottingham City was quick and quiet. It was quick because they wanted to get rid of me as fast as possible. It was quiet because we flew over the thousands of huge bubbles that made up the busy DeVanter Mining Enterprises. And as we flew over them the Arbos feasted their eyes on their new holdings.

Aunt Katherine sat in the back with me, her eyes half closed. I could tell that her data was starting to run low again. All I could do was hope there would be enough to keep her going in the terminal. There no way I could rescue her real self without having her dummy along.

73

Not that I had a real plan. I didn't. I knew where I wanted to end up, but I still didn't know exactly how to get there.

In a little while the gold towers and ramps of Nottingham City appeared on the Alpha I horizon. Somewhere in that city, and, I hoped, in the VOYA-CODE terminal, my real Aunt Katherine was sleeping. I had to find her. And I had to wake her up.

"We're almost there, Master Jack," Frank Arbo said.

"I see it, thanks."

We had to stay "friends" as long as possible.

Off to the right I saw a Superrocket landing. Coming in from Earth or Mars. *A safe way to travel,* I thought. *No bodies getting mixed up.*

Over the city the air buses and private craft filled the sky. Frank Arbo steered Aunt Katherine's solar craft skillfully, and soon we were over the center of the city. The VOYA-CODE terminal was at the very center, near the uni-

versity and the hospital. In fact, it looked like the hospital.

We set down on the roof, and Frank Arbo pressed the power panels and we stopped. A robot came out and gave us a parking card and then steered the craft into the garage.

We rode down to the Reception Area. The VOYA-CODE terminal here was bigger than the one back home.

A Reception-Microphone barred our way. Frank Arbo spoke into it. "Master Jack Stevenson returning to Earth," he said.

His voice activated a computer system; there were clicks and beeps and then a voice saying: "Proceed to Level 5, Room 5B. Alpha/Earth."

"They're expecting you, Master Jack," Frank said, beaming at me.

"Oh, we hope you have a pleasant trip, Master Jack," Ruth Arbo said.

Aunt Katherine said nothing. She was walking like a sleepwalker. *Don't give out, Aunt Katherine,* I begged her silently. *I need you, old girl.*

Level 5 was filled with travelers on their way to other galaxies. Or just arriving. At one end of a large central room was a small gift shop. I stared at it. That was it. Now I knew what I had to do.

I stopped walking, like a little kid.

"Come along, Master Jack," Frank Arbo said. "Your trip is scheduled to depart in ten minutes."

"I just thought of something. I want a souvenir of Alpha to take back to Earth."

They looked surprised, as well they might. It was a very dumb thing to say.

Frank Arbo laughed. "Master Jack, it's quite impossible for you to take anything back, since you're not really going. Your real self never left Earth. You're only traveling by numbers."

"I don't care," I said stubbornly. "I want a souvenir to show my friends where I've been."

"That gift shop is for arriving travelers, Master Jack. Those who want to take presents to their Alpha hosts."

"I don't care. I want a souvenir."

Sometimes it pays to be only eleven years old.

Frank Arbo turned to Aunt Katherine. "Mrs. DeVanter, would you tell your nephew that such a thing is impossible?" He wasn't asking Aunt Katherine. He was ordering her.

"Such a thing is impossible," Aunt Katherine repeated so mechanically that the Arbos looked alarmed, afraid that I might notice something.

I was alarmed too. Aunt Katherine's

dummy didn't have much energy left. And I didn't have much time.

But I refused to budge.

Frank Arbo looked at his watch and they held a hurried conference. Then Ruth said, "All right, Master Jack, we'll buy you a souvenir rock of Alpha. And you can hold it while you start your trip."

"Thank you," I said.

"We'll be right back," Frank said, and he and Ruth headed for the gift shop at the other end of the room. They weren't going to wait

for me to pick the rock out. They were going to do that themselves.

I waited till there were people between us and them. Then I grabbed Aunt Katherine's hand.

"Come on, Aunt Katherine. We've got to hurry."

"Hurry where?" she asked, surprised.

"We've got to find your real you. It's got to be somewhere in this building, and we can't find it with the Arbos hanging around. Let's go!"

"Jack, I'm running down."

"You can do it, Aunt Katherine."

I gave a hard yank and she came with me. She was using up her last bit of energy, but she ran with me. She really was a grand old dummy.

10

THERE THEN BEGAN one of the craziest times in my life. Aunt Katherine and I raced up one escalator and down another trying to find Alpha/Earth Sleep-Storage before the Arbos found out we were gone.

We ran from one waiting room into another: into Alpha/Uranus, then Alpha/Mars, then Alpha/Kappa, Saturn, Beta World.

People stared at us as we ran. Nobody in a VOYA-CODE terminal runs for anything. There's nothing to catch. The trip can't take place without the Traveler.

"Jack," puffed Aunt Katherine, "I can't keep this up."

"Just a little longer, Aunt Katherine. It's got to be around here somewhere."

If I could find the Alpha/Earth waiting room, then it made sense that Sleep-Storage would be nearby. But where was the waiting room? And maybe Sleep-Storage *wouldn't* be nearby. I'd have to ask someone. I didn't want to take the time to ask. But I'd have to.

A Travel Attendant in a white uniform came out of an unmarked room. She was carrying papers in one hand.

"Miss," I said, "could you tell me where I can find the storage place for Alpha-to-Earth Travelers?"

"You're not permitted in here, young man," she snapped.

In *here?* I stared at the unmarked door.

"Ah, Master Jack," said a voice behind me.

It was Frank Arbo, and behind him was Ruth Arbo.

"C'mon, Aunt Katherine," I said, and yanked her sideways into the room the Travel Attendant had just come out of.

"Stop!" the Travel Attendant shouted.

"You're not allowed in there. It's forbidden. It's—"

I shut the door and locked it, fast.

We were in darkness. I could hear Aunt Katherine breathing hard beside me.

There was a banging on the door.

I ignored it.

As our eyes got used to the dark, I saw that we were in a different kind of room than any I'd been in before. A large room, and there was a bluish light off to one side.

"Come on, Aunt Katherine."

"Jack, I'm afraid."

"There's nothing to be afraid of," I lied.

"I'm so tired. I don't think I can take another step."

"Sure you can. We'll walk together."

There was more pounding on the door. We ignored it and walked slowly across the large room toward the bluish light.

When we got there, we saw a strange sight. There were dozens of small cubicles— little glass rooms—and inside the rooms were beds, and on the beds were people sleeping.

Behind us there was an even louder banging on the door. It sounded as if more people than the Arbos were trying to get in.

In front of us—silence. People asleep. Voyagers to a distant planet called Earth.

Holding Aunt Katherine's hand, making her take just one step at a time, I looked into each little room.

In the first cubicle an older man was snoozing, a big smile on his face. He looked like a businessman on a trip to Earth. *His dummy must be making a lot of sales,* I thought.

In the next cubicle, a boy my age was sleeping on his side. He was grinning too. He looked as though he had been sent to Earth for a vacation and he was having a great time.

In the next cubicle, a young woman was frowning in her sleep. Someone on Earth must have been giving her a hard time. Or maybe she was giving him a hard time.

Next there was a couple who looked like a husband and wife. They were very well dressed. They must have taken an expensive tour somewhere.

In the next cubicle, a little kid was sleeping happily.

Next there was a mailman, probably checking on a lost letter to Wyoming.

In the next cubicle—I stopped breathing. There, lying there, looking very grim, was the person who was also, at this moment, standing next to me—Aunt Katherine.

"Look," I said to her.

She looked. She turned pale.

"It's me."

"It's your real self, that's who it is. Now we've got to find somebody to show you both to."

But we didn't have to find anybody. They found us. The pounding behind us had stopped as someone unlocked the door. Into Alpha/Earth Storage came not only the Arbos but an Alpha policeman and the Travel Attendant, and a tall man in a white coat that had a big button on it that read: VOYA-CODE DIRECTOR, ALPHA GALAXY.

The Director said, "What is going on here? You have no business being in here."

"I do, but my dummy Aunt Katherine doesn't," I said. "Her real self is lying in that room, which means that she is supposed to be on a VOYA-CODE trip to Earth."

The Director looked from my dummy aunt to my real aunt asleep in the cubicle.

"This," he said indignantly, "is highly illegal."

"And this isn't the half of it. These two people—Frank and Ruth Arbo—must have gone to Earth and brought my dummy aunt back and programmed her to give away all her property to them."

"Oh, Master Jack," said Frank, "how can you say such a terrible thing?"

"It's all a mistake, sir," Ruth Arbo said to the Director.

"No one is to leave the terminal until we get to the bottom of this," the Director said.

He ordered that my aunt's VOYA-CODE travel records be brought and that Aunt Katherine herself be taken from storage into a recovery room. A few minutes later we all crowded in there, and while the Director ex-

amined the travel records, the Travel Attendant woke up the real Aunt Katherine.

First one eye opened and then the other. And there was Aunt Katherine looking up at the faces looking down on her. The first face she saw was mine.

"Jack Stevenson," she exclaimed, "it's about time I got to this silly old planet of yours. I feel like I've been traveling forever."

The next people she saw were the Arbos. She looked astonished.

"What are you two doing here? You're supposed to be back on Alpha looking after my mines."

That, and the travel records, were all the VOYA-CODE Director needed. He ordered the Arbos arrested on the spot. Then he explained, apologetically, to Aunt Katherine: "Ahem, you, uh, never did leave Alpha."

"Of course I never left," Aunt Katherine snapped. "That's the whole point of VOYA-CODE. I'm inside my dummy on Earth."

"I'm afraid, uh, dreadfully sorry, Mrs. De-

Vanter, but, ahem, your dummy is right here with you on Alpha."

And it was then that the real Aunt Katherine saw the dummy Aunt Katherine. The two Aunt Katherines stared at each other.

"Well," my real Aunt Katherine said, "this needs some explaining. I've never heard of such a thing. However, I can say it is a very beautiful likeness of me. A very handsome woman. How do you do?" she said to her dummy.

But my dummy Aunt Katherine didn't answer. She had finally and completely run out of data. Which was a good thing, because there wouldn't have been room for two Aunt Katherines on Alpha I.

11

"WELL, JACK," said Dad, "tell us about your trip to Alpha. And when can we expect Aunt Katherine on the Superrocket?"

We had just driven home from the VOYA-CODE terminal in New Jersey and were sitting around the living room. Mom, Dad, my sister Jan, and me.

"Dad, first of all, Aunt Katherine's not moving to Earth. And she's not going to sell her mines at all."

"What made her change her mind?" asked Mom.

"She didn't change her mind. She never intended to *move* here. She was only going to pay us a visit by VOYA-CODE."

"What?" they all said at once.

"It's a long story," I said.

"You'd better tell it to us," Jan said.

So I told Mom and Dad and Jan all about my trip to Alpha I, meeting Aunt Katherine, meeting the Arbos, finding out that Aunt Katherine was a dummy, figuring out how it had happened, and finally rescuing Aunt Katherine's real self.

When I was done, they were silent.

"That," said Mom, "is a horrible story. Why, you're lucky to be alive."

"We're proud of you, son," Dad said. And I knew he meant it.

"There's obviously a lot of tightening up to be done with this VOYA-CODE business," Dad went on. "They can't let their dummies be kidnapped and programmed by crooks. That's the most dangerous thing I've ever heard of in my life."

"I hope those Arbos are in jail right now."

"They are, Mom."

"Well, I don't want to be a pest, but I did tell Jack before he left that it was a weird way to travel."

"You were right, Jan," Mom said. "It turned out to be that and more. But if it hadn't been for Jack, who knows what would have happened to Aunt Katherine?"

"How is she now, Jack?"

"She's fine, Dad. She's taken control of the mining operations again and she says that by November she'll have everything in good shape. She's planning on visiting us for Christmas."

"She'll never make it here by Christmas," Jan said.

I grinned. "She's not coming by Super-rocket. She's going to take VOYA-CODE."

They looked shocked.

"Why?" Dad asked.

"She says it's the most restful way to travel."

Mom laughed first. And then we all did. It was funny. Then Dad said that Aunt Katherine was probably right. That despite its problems, VOYA-CODE was probably the way we'd all travel in the future. I agreed with

him. It had been a quick, safe trip back for
me.

Just to make sure, though, I sneaked my
hand around and touched the small of my
back.

It was nice and smooth.

7810

F
SLO

Slote, Alfred

My trip to Alpha I

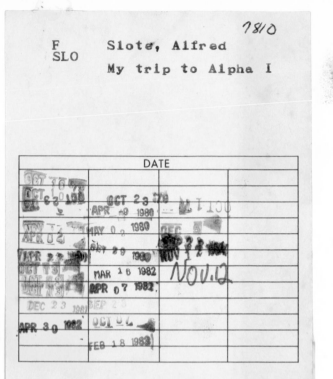

DATE			
OCT 16			
OCT 23	OCT 23		
	APR 9 1980		
NOV 12	MAY 03 1980	DEC	
APR 02	OCT 29 1980	NOV 12	
MAR 27		NOV 12	
OCT 13	MAR 16 1982		
OCT 28	APR 07 1982		
DEC 23 1981	SEP 23		
APR 30 1982	OCT 02		
	FEB 18 1983		